Owl Hawks

A Jack Cordell Western

R. Annan

WGA Reg. #: R31405 (5/12/2015)

eBook ISBN: 978-1-942338-21-5

Print Book ISBN: 978-1-942338-20-8

Jump into the adventures of Jack Cordell by R. Annan.

The Gunfighter in Winter

Long Ride to Hell's Kitchen

Owl Hawks

Gunfight at Barfield Springs

Shootout at Sanctuary City

Last Days of a Gunfighter (*forthcoming*)

Coming soon: Clay Jared Westerns

To

A Soldier and a Patriot

Sergeant Major Anthony R. Annan, USA, Retired

Rancher Cal Venters was a problem solver.

When his cowhands kept getting the tar beat out of them in the Skinny Lady Saloon, Venters had a solution in mind. At a cattle convention in Chicago he found Arny Trask, a bare-knuckle boxer, and brought him back to the Circle V to learn the ways of the cowboy. Of course he had to pay Arny a lot more than this other hands, but Venters felt he was a good investment, if used properly.

He left that part up to his ramrod, Slinger Barlow, and Slinger knew just what to do with Arny Trask.

On a cold, crisp February evening, Barlow and Trask walked slowly into the Skinny Lady Saloon. It was Friday and the place was packed with cowhands from the other ranches looking to gamble, get drunk, find a girl, or all three.

As they went past a table where three cowboys from the Flying G ranch sat joking Trask purposely brushed up against it and knocked over a bottle of whiskey, sending it rolling off onto the floor. One of the Flying G cowboys jumped up and confronted Trask.

"Hey, fellah! Watch where the hell yer goin'!"

Trask smiled and pulled his kid gloves tighter on his fists. He sniffed the air and looked back at Barlow, chuckling.

"Say, boss, I smell dog-shit, don't you?" He then shoved the Flying G man backwards, sending him falling over his chair.

The second cowboy, a short, stocky man, jumped up and swung a haymaker at Trask's jaw. Trask brushed it aside and smashed the cowboy's nose in with a stiff right. The third cowboy waded in to help his friend, his fists flying. Trask hit him with a vicious uppercut and dropped him like a sack of potatoes, breaking his jaw. The first cowboy started to get up but Trask caught him on his knees and clubbed him senseless with a right and a left to the face.

Slinger Barlow looked around the barroom, with a sneer on his lips. All eyes were on him and Trask. The place was suddenly very quiet.

"Anybody else?" Barlow asked. No one answered. He tossed a double eagle on the table. "Fer the spilt rotgut, boys."

He nodded to Arny Trask and they headed for the door. Barlow had done what he came to do and that was to put the fear of the Circle V into every cowpoke in the valley, and he had just done that.

On the way out they bumped into two cowboys, Bob Harnell and Rudy Adams.

Harnell and Trask stood face-to-face, taking each other's measure. It looked like a fight but Harnell smiled and stepped aside. As Trask went by, Harnell shoulder-butted him up against Barlow. Barlow grunted and swore.

Trask and Harnell were inches apart when Trask backed off to throw a punch. Barlow grabbed his arm and stopped him.

"Not now," Barlow said. "We'll get him later."

Trask smiled at Harnell. "I'll take care of you some other time, cowboy!" He followed Barlow outside. In moments they were riding away.

Bob Harnell was a young cowboy who rode for the Bar T brand and Rudy Adams rode for the Bar J. They got a bottle of rotgut and two glasses and looked for an empty table. They finally found one and sat down.

With Trask and Barlow gone, things got loud and raucous again. The three beat-up cowboys left to see Doc Arnold. Adams and Harnell sat quietly drinking. They weren't there to have fun. Their minds were mostly on water and grass.

"It just ain't right," Adams said. "Venters shouldn't have all thet much power."

Harnell nodded and took a drink of whiskey and shivered. Both the Bar T and the Bar J were just small spreads compared to Cal Venter's huge Circle V ranch.

"He puts up a fence any darn place he feels like and nobody kin do anything ta stop him. It ain't right. He's got most all the water 'n grass boxed in fer himself," Adams said.

"Yeah, and it's all free range, too," Harnell complained. "He takes what he wants fer himself. He don't give a damn about the small ranches."

Just then Curt Lambeth of the Circle F, Wes Stoner of the Leaning R, Ben Madden of the Circle B, and Tim Husker of the Flying G came into the saloon. They dodged their way over to the bar and got a bottle of rotgut and four glasses. Lambeth looked around and saw Adams and Harnell. He motioned to the others and they walked slowly over to join them.

"What the heck are you two lookin' so sour about?" Lambeth asked.

"We was jest sayin' how Venters has taken over the valley fer his own," Adams said.

Stoner pulled the cork from the bottle and poured his comrades a drink. They tossed it down, shivered and grunted.

"This stuff keeps a gitin' worse," Husker groaned. "I wonder who's a makin' it?"

"It tastes worse than Doc Arnold's embalmin' fluid!" Madden chuckled.

"About Venters," Lambeth said, returning to the subject at hand. "He sure thinks he's the kingpin around these here parts, don't he?"

"Well, he cut the Bar T off from prime grazin' land," Harnell said. "Bar T cattle is starvin' because of him."

"That ain't right," Stoner complained.

"No, it ain't, an' something sure oughtta be done about it," Madden interjected.

"I hear him and his son Todd don't get along," Husker said.

"He's a wild one, that Todd," Adams reflected.

"Yeah," Madden said, "I hear him and the old man fight day and night."

Harnell said, "I kinda feel sorry fer the kid. We met a couple of times. He ain't like his old man."

They drank a while in silence under the sputtering oil lamp. Cigarette smoke curled around their hats.

"Talking about fencin' people in," Stoner said. "They tried that on a spread I rode fer up in Wyomin' territory."

"Fences?" Adams asked.

"Yeah," Stoner said. "But we had a cure fer it." He took another drink.

"There ain't no cure fer Venters," Madden said. "He's got everybody runnin' with their tails between their legs. His ramrod, Slinger Barlow? Man, he's one mean son of a bitch!"

"He sure is," Husker said. "An' he's damn fast on the draw, too. The quickest in the valley."

"He sure is," Harnell said.

Adams chuckled. "Hell, why do you think Venters hired him? An' thet kid from Chicago? Harnell shoulder-butted him up agin Barlow and fer a minute it looked like a fight was gonna break out!"

Stoner whistled. "Lucky fer you, Harnell! You don't wantta mess with Arny Trask. He's a boxer."

"Hell, I'll jest kick him in the balls," Harnell chuckled.

"So, Stoner," Lambeth said, "what was thet cure fer puttin' up fences you was talking about?"

"There's only one cure fer Venters, and that's gunplay," Husker said.

"I ain't talkin' about no gun play," Stoner said, "I'm a talkin' about somethin' different."

"Yeah? We'll what's that?" Adams asked.

Stoner took a drink and started to roll a cigarette. The others waited.

"Well, spit it out, Stoner," Madden said.

"In Wyomin' when the cattlemen tried ta close off the free range, strange things happened."

"Like what?" Adams asked.

"Like fences a comin' down in the night, thet's what."

"They did?" Madden said.

"They sure as hell did. Big holes started to pop up all along the fence lines," Stoner said.

"Who'd do such a thing as that?" Harnell asked.

"The Owl Hoots, thet's who," Stoner chuckled.

"The Owl Hoots? Who the heck are the Owl Hoots?"

"I ain't a sayin'. All I know is they did it."

"Was you one a them?" Harnell asked.

"I ain't a sayin'," Stoner said again, evasively. "All I'm a sayin' is thet five er six good men kin pull down a quarter mile of fence in no time."

"You son of a gun!" Husker chuckled. "You were one of them, wasn't you? You were a Hoot Owl."

"It ain't Hoot Owl, Husker," Stoner said. "It's Owl Hoots."

"An' you was one of them, wasn't you?" Lambeth chortled. "I kin see it in yer face, Stoner!"

Stoner took a drink and smiled. "Maybe, maybe not. I ain't sayin'."

"Wouldn't it be somethin' if ol' Cal Venter's fences started comin' all apart on him?" Lambeth chuckled.

"Yeah, wouldn't that be a hoot!" Harnell laughed.

"Now, who'd do setch a thing as thet ta ol' Cal Venters fences?" Husker asked jokingly.

"Nobody I know of," Madden chuckled.

"I bet Stoner knows somebody like thet, right Stoner, you old Owl Hooter!"

"An' ifn they did, they wouldn't call themselves no stupid Owl Hoots," Lambeth said. "Maybe Owl Hawks, but not Owl Hoots."

"Yeah," Adams said. "I like thet, Owl Hawks."

They all fell silent for a moment, listening to the loud noises around them.

"Did they, like, wear masks?" Harnell asked.

"Yeah," Stoner said, "stockin' masks, as I heard."

They were silent again. Suddenly Madden said to Harnell, "You say Venters has cut the Bar T off from grass?"

"Yep, he sure has," Harnell said.

"He's done it to the Flyin' G, too," Husker said.

"And the Circle F," Lambeth added.

"Well, thet ain't right," Madden said. It was meant for all of them. They nodded. "Stoner, I think you jest opened up a hornet's nest with yer talk about Hoot Owls an' such stuff. Are you all talk, or what?"

"I ain't a scared of Venters or Slinger Barlow, if thet's what yer askin'," Stoner said.

"I ain't scared of them, either," Lambeth said.

Suddenly Madden stood up and grabbed the bottle of whiskey and walked out into the night. Harnell and Adams got their bottle and left, too. The others quickly followed.

It was cool and dark outside. They mounted up and rode into the night without saying a word.

Suddenly, one of them gave off what sounded like a very loud owl's hoot.

"Stoner, you crazy son of a bitch!" Husker whispered.

"Come on, boys, let's hear it!" Stoner yelled.

Suddenly they all started hooting like an owl. The sound carried far in the cool February air.

They rode on.

2.

When Todd Venters was fifteen years old his father yanked him out of school and handed him over to Slinger Barlow. Barlow, a rough and tough cowboy, was the ramrod of Cal Venter's Circle V spread. For the next year or so, Todd would be under his wing, learning how to be a true cowboy.

The boy's father threw him out of the house and had him live with the cowhands down at the bunkhouse. At first Todd grudgingly took to their ways, including swearing, telling tall tales, playing cards, and scratching his butt. He tried chewing tobacco but quickly abandoned that habit. Nor did he smoke.

The Circle V cowhands came to like the kid and admired the way he would get back on a horse after being thrown, kicked, and bitten. They also felt sorry for him because of his hot-tempered father. There was something wrong in the Venter's family, but they knew better than to talk.

The boy went on his first cattle drive at the age of seventeen, a year before the state of Kansas put a ban on

Texas cattle, which it did to protect its own cattle business. This forced the railroads to later build lines directly south into Texas.

Several herds left the Dark Valley River Basin, one after the other. Cal Venters himself led the Circle V herd on the trek across the Cimarron River north to Ellsworth, a two to three week cattle drive, depending on the weather.

Once on the trail, Slinger Barlow kept the boy at arm's length. He was no baby-sitter, and didn't want the kid too close to him and his clique of cowhands. They liked their privacy.

Young Todd's first job was as a swing rider. He rode up and down outside the herd to catch strays in trouble. He and three other cowboys had their hands full pulling cows out of the mud, quicksand, or thorn bushes.

After that he was a flank rider, staying with the herd, keeping it moving at a steady pace and keeping it tight at night. Nights seemed to drag endlessly on, and he was glad to see the sun come up and smell the coffee, bacon, and sourdough biscuits cooking.

Then came the job of drag rider, urging the slower cattle along to catch up with the others. This was just as boring as the other jobs. Todd began to think being a cowboy wasn't all it was cracked up to be.

The final job Todd had was with the remuda master who had charge of the horses, over three hundred of them. Todd had noticed that the horses tired easily on a grass diet as opposed to oats and hay. A cowboy sometimes had to change horses twice or even three time a day. The exhausted ones were roped off from the others, and given time to rest.

Young Todd Venters came to learn a lot about the cowboys themselves. He found some to be simple minded, and childish in their ways. Though uneducated, they were honest, generous, and hard working. For the most part, they were poor, so poor many didn't even own a horse or saddle. It was provided by the ranchers. Generally all they had was a saddlebag to indicate they were cowboys.

In spite of all this, the average cowboy had a very deep respect and reverence for women. And they were devoted to the brand they rode for. They would fight and often die for it.

But not all cowboys were like that.

A few who came west after the Civil War were cold and calculating and had dark thoughts. They might be laying low, or hiding out, or waiting for a chance to take advantage of their employers. These men couldn't be trusted. When the chips were down, when things got hard, they would strike down their employers or perhaps just ride off and desert them.

Todd Venters rubbed elbows with both types of cowboys.

Days on the trail drive seemed long and tedious. The young boy sometimes spent ten to twelve hours a day in the saddle. His body hardened, his hands blistered, and his back ached, but he never complained. He wouldn't give his father the pleasure of seeing his pain. Cal Venters would pass by his son and never even glance his way.

Todd didn't care for Slinger Barlow so he stayed away from him. He made close friends with the other cowboys and eventually he came to know most of them by name, even the cowboys covering the other herds. He played cards with them whenever he had free time. Everyone liked Todd Venters, but few liked his father or Slinger Barlow.

That was the first and last trail drive for Todd Venters. The following year the Kansas ban went into effect, and the era of the long cattle drives came to an end.

After that came the fence war in the Dark River Valley Basin. It was started by Cal Venters who fenced off water and grass as the cattle count on the Circle V grew larger and larger. The smaller ranchers could only sit helplessly by and watch.

With the cattle drive finished, young Todd Venters had returned a different person. He was now his own man and could stand on his own two feet. He did miss the excitement and friendship of the drive, but was glad to be home in the valley. Many a night he had lain on the hard ground, under the stars, thinking of a girl he had seen many times at school but had never been introduced to. He hoped someday he would see her again.

Now that the trail drive was over, perhaps he would.

3.

At age fifty-five, six-foot-four, granite faced Cal Venters was a very imposing figure. He had a full head of solid black hair and a flowing beard. It framed his face, making him look like a biblical patriarch, broad- shouldered and powerful. His skin was browned by the weather and his big hands were calloused and strong from work. But it was his deep set eyes that made his enemies cringe in fear. When old Cal Venters was angry his eyes seemed to glow and burn with a raging fire.

The Venters were one of the first families to come to the Dark River Valley in the early days. Some settlers were farmers and some were cattlemen. The land was free to hold and there was more than enough for the twenty families that came in. They formed an Association and everyone got along together. They fought off rustlers and marauders and helped each other in times of draught, and locust and grasshopper invasions. Their children went to the same schools and the same church.

All conflicts were settle peaceably.

But somewhere along the way Cal Venters changed. Whenever a fellow farmer or rancher fell on bad times, Cal was right there to buy him out, instead of helping him.

"You don't want some carpet bagger comin' in here buyin' us all out, now do ya, Del? Of course not!" So Dell sold out to his good friend Cal Venters, at a loss.

Venters also had a contact at the Jaggersville Bank who let him know who was behind on mortgage payments, and who was about to be foreclosed on. That made it easy for him to get in a first offer. Some of the small ranchers got into trouble at the poker table and couldn't pay their monthly bank payments. Venters came in and settled for them, then send them packing after he bought out their debt from the bank.

Now there was no more vacant land left in the valley. Venters had swallowed up all the free range by buying most of the small ranches. Now, instead of twenty families, there was just Venters and nine small ones. Venters owned more than half the Dark River Valley and was slowly fencing it off. He had his loyal ramrod Slinger Barlow and a small army of fifty cowhands to back him up. No one had the resources or the nerve to go up against Cal Venters.

Cal Venter's wife was a petite demure woman of high breeding. She ran a tight house and she was the only one who was able to calm the big man down when he was in a fit of rage. One touch of her little hand and Cal would begin to purr like a kitten. Beth Venter's was tiny, had sparkling blue eyes and everyone in the Valley loved and respected her. She played the piano and sang for visitors. Beth was the big man's pride and joy, and he loved to show her off.

When his wife became with child, Venters was very happy and when the doctor said there might be twins he was ecstatic. But the pregnancy did not go well. The first child was still born and the second of the twins caused problems.

Beth suffered a painful complicated delivery that almost ended her life. It took all of Doc Arnold's skill to pull her through. It took her a long time to recover. They had to get a woman from town to nurse Todd, the surviving twin.

For some reason Cal Venters could never bring himself to love the boy. In his mind, Todd had tried to kill his mother. She never regained her health. In his father's eyes it was all Todd's fault. Knowing he could never earn his father's love and respect, the boy became rebellious and cold.

They fought constantly. Todd returned his father's hate ounce for ounce, pound for pound.

One day Todd Venters saw seventeen-year old Fanny Templeton. Her mother, Ella Templeton, owned the small Bar T ranch that was flanked by his father's Circle V. Fanny sat across from her mother as she drove her buckboard up from Donner's Mercantile.

It was a late Saturday morning, clear and sunny. Todd and three of the Circle V cowboys had been drinking at the Skinny Lady, in Jaggersville, all night. They were out on the street horsing around and wrestling. One of the cowboys fired off a shot. Mrs. Templeton's horse bolted. It came straight at them up the road.

Everyone scattered except young Todd. He stood frozen like a deer stuck on a track watching the train coming at him. Just as the buckboard was upon him, Todd jumped sideways and grabbed the horse's bridle and hung on while the animal dragged him fifty feet up the road and stopped. He petted it and whispered to it, calming it down.

"Thank you," Ella Templeton said. "You're Cal Venter's boy, aren't you?"

Fanny stared at the handsome boy.

"Yes ma'am," Todd said. He was overwhelmed by the beauty of both mother and daughter. "I'm Todd, the black sheep of the family."

Ella Templeton smiled sympathetically. "You look all worn out, Mr. Venters. Perhaps you and your friends should go home and get some rest."

Todd Venters let the words go in one ear and out the other. With his mouth open wide and his eyes gawking stupidly, he came around the buckboard to get a better look at Fanny. He stood as if struck dumb by her beauty.

Finally Fanny Templeton giggled and turned to her mother and said, "He's crazy, momma. We better go before he starts barking like a dog!"

"My warmest regards to your mother, Mr. Venters," Ella Templeton said as she snapped the reins.

The buckboard moved off leaving Todd Venters standing slack-jawed in the middle of the road. He suddenly howled like a wounded coyote. He put a hand over his heart and fell backwards on the ground. His three friends ran over to him and looked down.

"What's wrong with you, Todd?" one asked.

"I been shot by the arrow of love," the young man moaned.

"Who was that looker?" another asked.

"That was Miss Fanny Templeton." Todd said, sitting up. "I went to school with her as a kid but I ain't seen her in a coon's age."

"Well, she sure ain't no kid anymore," the third one said.

"Yeah, I noticed," young Todd said. "I surely did!"

4.

A week after the buckboard incident, Todd Venters rode across Bar T land and sat in his saddle on a knoll above the Templeton ranch house. He stared down at the white sheets that sparkled and snapped like sails on a ship in the wind. He came there every day for the last three days, hoping to get a glimpse of Fanny Templeton. Now it was washday and she stood there in all her glory hanging out wet bedsheets to dry.

He dismounted and walked his horse slowly down to where she was. He stood there watching the breezes playing with her yellow tresses.

"I saw you up there," she said. "You aimin' ta kill me, crazy man?"

"I aim ta kiss you," he said.

Fanny chuckled. "You were wild in school, and yer sure wild now, Todd Venters."

"Kin I kiss ya, Fanny Templeton?"

"You better not try. I'll scream, if you do."

"Then I will not attempt to do thet 'till you ask me to."

"Well, I wouldn't hold my breath, ifn I was you, Todd Venters."

Suddenly the boy's horse nudged his shoulder, pushing her closer to Fanny Templeton. She giggled.

"What' he tryin' ta do?"

"He wants ta see us a kissin', is what."

"What's his name?"

"Tumbleweed."

"He's kinda friendly, ain't he?"

"Not ta everyone," Todd said. Then. "You wanna take a ride sometime?"

"Alone? Jest you an' me?"

"Sure, I won't eat ya."

Fanny thought about that for a moment. "Maybe. I'd have to ask my mom, first."

"You do thet."

"She's a watchin' you right now, with a shotgun," Fanny chuckled.

"Oh! In thet case I'd best be a moseyin' along then, Miss Templeton," the boy said. He mounted up. "You got anything to say ta me before I go?"

Fanny said nothing but as he rode off she called, "I'll be ready fer a ride tomorrow, if ya come 'n git me!"

"Same time?"

She nodded and waved. He rode away over the knoll.

Fanny carried the empty wash basket into the kitchen. Her mother was working over a large pot of stew at the cast iron stove.

"I was talkin' to crazy Todd Venters," Fanny said.

"I know, dear," Ella Templeton said. "He's nice, but maybe you shouldn't get too friendly with him."

"Why not?"

"Well, his father is not going to let anything happen between you two."

"Why not?"

"The Venters don't mix with other people."

"Is that all?"

Ella looked at her daughter and sighed.

25

"His mother is nice enough, but his father is not well liked in the valley," she said.

"What's thet got ta do with Todd and me?"

"Nothing, I guess, except that his father has us all but shut in with his fences, dear. Sooner or later the small ranchers are going to have to do something about it."

"What are they gonna do?"

"I don't know," Ella said. She sounded uncertain. "I guess there isn't much we can do."

"He wants ta see me agin momma, and I wanna see him, too."

Ella sighed and hugged her daughter. "All I'm sayin' is don't get your hopes up too high."

"Alright, momma, I won't."

Ella Templeton gave her daughter a reassuring hug.

5.

They met one balmy, cool March day on the old coach road where it ran along the Pecos River above Santa Fe.

"Where you heading, kid?" the stranger asked. He wore a suit and gun, an indication that he was probably a gambler.

"Nowhere in particular, mister."

The stranger nodded. The kid wasn't a talker and that was just fine. He wasn't interested in other people's problems. If the kid was on the run, he didn't want to know that either. He had already met too many drifters in the past. Some of them were trouble, and trouble was the last thing the stranger needed right now.

They rode together in the chilly afternoon with the wind in their faces, their hats pulled low. What had started out as a nice day had turned dark and gray.

Finally, up ahead, they saw the lights of a town.

"What's thet?" the kid asked.

"Jaggersville," the stranger said.

The kid nodded. The stranger had already noticed he carried an old 1862, .36 center-fire Army revolver. It was rare, but seemed well cared for.

They entered Jaggersville, Texas and parted company. The stranger rode on to the Skinny Lady Saloon near midtown, and the kid stopped at a gun shop. He went in and took his gun from its holster and laid it on the counter.

"What's it worth?" he asked.

The owner, an old man with glasses, picked up the revolver and inspected it closely. He opened the cylinder, removed the bullets, then closed and spun it, listening to the sound it made. He pulled the trigger.

"Nice action, son," the old man said."

"It's been modified. It belonged to my dad."

"Confederate?" The boy nodded. "You passin' through are you?" the man asked.

"Yeah, I guess," the young man said.

The old man put the gun on the counter. He reached under it and came up with four eagles. He laid them next to the gun and stared at the boy.

The young man nodded. "Sure." He scooped the money up and put it in his pocket.

The old man looked sad. He'd seen this before. Young cowboys down on their luck, selling their guns and getting drunk to drown their cares and woes.

"It'll be here if you want it back," the old man said. The kid nodded and left the shop.

Outside the kid grabbed his horse's reins and led him along the street. He saw the stranger's horse up ahead, in front of the saloon. He tied his next to it and went in.

The place was busy. Cigarette smoke and the stink of stale tobacco juice permeated the air. It was heavy enough to get into the pores. There was also the ever-present aroma of whiskey. Oil lamps hung at intervals from the rafters, casting flickering shadows.

The kid looked around, saw the stranger at a table, and walked slowly over. It was full, so he waited until a man dropped out. He took the empty chair between the stranger and a cowboy. The stranger didn't look directly at him, but saw that the kid no longer had his gun. In a place like this, that was a big mistake. Just looking at someone the wrong way could make them angry enough to take a shot at you. When that happened, you'd best have a gun.

There were a total of five players at the table now. The stranger, the kid, the cowboy, the town lawyer named Eli Meyers, and the town doctor named Seth Arnold.

"It's poker, kid," the stranger said. The kid nodded.

The lawyer dealt and won a hand. Next the doc won a hand, and then the stranger won a hand. The cowboy did well but by the fifth hand, the kid was flat broke. He started to get up.

"Stick around, kid." The stranger pushed ten eagles in front of him. The kid shrugged and sat down.

The game went on. The kid played it safe and dropped out when his cards were bad. After a few hands he felt his luck begin to change. He won a few pots, tossed in a few hands, then felt it again and started on a winning streak.

He was well ahead when it happened.

There were five Circle V cowboys at the next table. They had been baiting and agitating everyone around them with bad talk and remarks. Most people ignored or put up with it. Suddenly, one noticed the lawyer. That man was Arny Trask. He looked over at Eli Meyers and chuckled.

"Hey, Eli! Been cheatin' any old widows' outta their savin's lately?" Trask yelled over.

Eli Meyers glanced across at Trask, and said, "Settle down now, Arny."

Meyers turned back to his cards. He looked at the kid and smiled. "Where are you from, young man?"

"Wyomin', sir," the kid said.

Suddenly Trask got up and walked over and stared at the cowboy. "I was hopin' to run into you again, Harnell. You remember me, ass hole?" Trask was wearing twin Colts.

"Oh, yeah," Harnell said. "I butted yer city ass up agin yer boss, Slinger Barlow, a while back."

"And now here you are," Trask chuckled.

"Yep, here I am, Chicago," Harnell said calmly.

"I'll take care of you in a minute," Trask said. Then he looked at the kid. "You from Wyoming, kid?"

Slinger Barlow had been teaching Trask the quick draw and Trask was aching to try it out on someone. The kid looked like an easy target.

"Yep," the kid said, studying his cards.

"I thought I smelled sheep shit," Trask said.

Suddenly everyone at the table stared at the kid, waiting for his answer.

The kid smiled and said, "That's yer own breath yer a smellin', friend." He put his cards face down on the table and looked at Trask. The stranger chuckled.

"Who the hell you laughin' at, gambler?" Trask growled at the stranger. "I'll kick yer ass, too!"

"Behave now, Mr. Trask," Eli Meyers said.

"Who the hell you tellin' to behave, shyster?" Trask sneered.

He took off his hat and swung it against the back of the lawyer's head, knocking his glasses off. They hit the table and lay there. Eli Meyers slowly put them back on.

"Arny," the doctor said. "You should go home."

"Who asked you, Doc?" Trask said. He suddenly glared at Harnell. "When I'm finished with sheep-boy here, I'll take care of you, ass hole!" He glanced at the stranger. "I'll settle with you last, mister."

"Bring it on, friend," Harnell chuckled.

The other Circle V cowboys got up and came over to stand alongside Trask.

"Havin' trouble, Arny?" one asked.

Trask chuckled. "I got me a smart ass sheep dipper from Wyomin' thet don't know when to keep his trap shut, Bill."

One of the other Venter's men noticed the lawyer and the doc and grabbed Trask by the arm. "Come on, Arny," he said. "We don't want no trouble now, do we?"

"Don't touch me, Fred!"

"Sure, sure, Arny," Fred said and backed away with a worried look on his face.

Trask nodded at the kid. "Eat them words kid or else I'll---"

"Or you'll what," the kid said smoothly, "crap yer pants?"

This last remark had Trask foaming at the mouth. "You son of a bitch, I'm gonna ventilate you good! Draw!"

"Stop it, Trask. He's not armed!" the doctor said.

"Well, I'll count ta three an' he better be on his feet and runnin' fer the door, then!" Trask yelled.

"I don't run from fence menders," the kid said.

"Then yer gonna die right here an' now!" Trask growled.

Arny Trask went for his twin Colts but never made it. A gun barked and his body jerked as if struck in the chest by a sledgehammer. He fell back into the arms of one of the Circle V cowboys. His gun hands hung limp at his sides, his twin Colts lay on the floor.

People scattered into the shadows of the saloon. The lawyer crouched sideways in his chair as the doctor slid down low in his. The stranger held his gun up above the table, covering the other Venter's men who had drawn their weapons.

"Don't try it!" he said. They put their guns back.

The kid was on his feet holding the gun that Harnell had slipped to him under the table. No one moved or spoke for a moment.

"When Venters hears of this, you're a dead man, Wyomin'," one of Venters' men finally said. "And you too, Harnell! And you, mister!" He pointed at the stranger.

"Here comes Marshal Spears!" someone yelled.

The stranger put his gun away. He picked up his money and the others did the same. The game was over and Eli Meyers put the cards back in the box. A bunch of cowboys gathered around to get a look at the kid.

The Marshal, a tall gaunt, middle-aged man, came up to the table. He looked at Venters' cowhands and then at the others.

"What happened, Doc?"

"It was fair and square," the doctor said. "Self-defense, Marshal. You can ask anyone here."

"That's right, Marshal," the lawyer said.

"Who are you, mister?" the Marshal asked scrutinizing the stranger closely.

"Nobody, Marshal."

"Got a name?"

"Brazos."

The Marshall stared hard at the stranger for a moment. His concentration was broken by the doctor's voice.

"Mr. Brazos was a big help in preventing further bloodshed, Marshal."

Marshal Spears stroked his chin and nodded. He turned to the Venters' cowboys. "You had best get him back to the Circle V, boys."

They nodded and grabbed Trask's body and carried him outside. In a few minutes they were riding away.

"I'll take my gun back now, kid," Harnell said. "By the way, my name is Harnell, Bob Harnell. I ride for the Bar T."

"My name is Ed Cole and thanks for slippin' me the gun, Harnell."

"My pleasure, Cole."

"We'll have to make a report out," the Marshal said. They followed him out of the Skinny Lady Saloon.

After giving a deposition at the Marshal's office, they stood outside talking. The kid took his winnings out of his pocket and handed the stranger ten double eagles.

"Thanks for the loan, Mr. Brazos," Ed Cole said.

"Sure, Wyoming," Brazos said, taking the money. "So long, kid. Stay out of trouble." He walked up the road towards the hotel.

"Mr. Brazos," the lawyer and the doc yelled after him. "Do you have a moment?" They hurried to catch up with him.

Ed Cole shook Bob Harnell's hand. "You sure saved my bacon, Harnell," he said. He was still a little shook up over the shooting. "If you hadn't slipped me that Colt I'd be dead as a doornail right now.' I sure owe you a lot."

"You sure do, Wyomin'," Harnell said, "an' yer gonna pay me back, right now."

"Oh? How's thet?"

"By signin' on to ride fer the Bar T."

"Punchin' cows?"

"Yeah, an' a lot more, too. I'll tell you on the way out."

"It sounds mysterious."

"However it sounds, it ain't as dull as punchin' cows," Harnell chuckled.

The kid from Wyoming stared at the Bar T cowboy for a moment then shrugged. "Hell, why not? But I gotta go over to the gun shop 'n git my dad's gun back."

Harnell nodded and they started walking.

"Wait 'til you see Fanny Templeton and her mom," Harnell said. "They's the two prettiest women in the whole wide world."

The kid chuckled. "Is that why you work there?"

"Ain't that reason enough?" Harnell replied.

"I reckon," Cole said, slapping Harnell on the back.

6.

They brought the body of Arny Trask back to the Circle V Ranch. Cal Venters had them lay it on the dining room table for all to see.

"Who did it?" Venter's voice boomed around the room.

"Some kid, a sheep lover from Wyomin'," the one named Fred said.

"Did you get the bastard?" No one answered. "You four just stood there and let it happen?"

"The kid had help, Mr. Venters. Bob Harnell, a Bar T cowboy, and some other guy, a gambler," the cowboy called Bill said.

"And they're still alive and walkin' around?"

"Ah, yes sir."

"Arny Trask is dead and you four walk in here alive?" Cal Venters brought his fist down on the table next to the body. The table shook. He glared at them with eyes that blazed like burning coals.

The one called Fred started to speak. Venters cut him short, pointing towards the door.

"Get out! You're all finished! I don't want ta see any of you within fifty miles of the Circle V, ever! And don't bother to collect yer things. Just mount up and go! Now!" Venters' voice crashed like thunder throughout the house.

The cowboys left in a hurry.

Moments later, short burly Slinger Barlow came in. He greeted Venters and went over to the table and looked down at the body of Arny Trask. He turned to Venters.

"They did it again, boss," Barlow said in a rusty voice.

"The Owl Hawks?" Venters asked. Barlow nodded. "Where?"

"The D sector. They pulled down almost a half-mile of fence."

"We'll talk about that later, Barlow." Venters nodded at Trask's body. "Right now I want the bastards that killed Arny."

"Alright, sure, boss," Slinger Barlow said. "Any ideas about who did it?"

"A gambler, a kid from Wyomin', and Bob Harnell from the Bar T were in on it," Venters answered.

"Harnell, huh? It figures. Him and Arny didn't like each other. Arny was lookin' to brace him."

"The story is he slipped the kid a gun, under the table, at the Skinny Lady."

"The slick son of a bitch!"

"I want him taken care of, now!"

"Now? It's kinda late, ain't it, boss?"

"I don't care how late it is, Barlow! Get on it, now!"

"Sure, sure, boss. I'll take Singleton and Perry with me," the ramrod said. "Singleton is good with a gun and Perry is good with a knife."

"Start with the gambler," Venters said. "By now he's probably at the hotel with a whore."

Barlow chuckled. "They usually are, this time a night. I'll wait 'til after mid-night ta pay him a visit."

"What about the other two, the kid, and the Bar T cowboy?" Venters asked.

"I'm thinkin' maybe those two kin be found later at the Bar T, seein' as there are two pretty wimin out there." Barlow chuckled. "I wouldn't mind ramrodin' thet outfit myself."

"I'm sure you would," Venters said sarcastically. He didn't appreciate Barlow's brand of humor. "Make sure you do this right. I don't want any loose ends."

Barlow nodded and left. He just came back from the D sector and was tired. He cursed Venters under his breath and went to find Singleton and Perry.

Both men were down at the bunkhouse playing cards and drinking. They were in no condition to ride but he took them aside anyway He explained the situation to them and in half an hour they were riding out for Jaggersville in the cool dark night.

It was well after mid-night when they tied their horses in the alley next to the Royal Hotel. They saw the stranger's horse in front, at the rail. Evidently he had planned to move on in the morning or his horse would be down at the stables. They went into the empty lobby.

The sign-in register was laying on the counter next to a flickering oil lamp. Barlow looked at the names. Mr. Brazos was the last to sign in. He signed into room number six.

Singleton and Perry followed their boss up the stairs to the second floor landing. They soon found the room. Singleton tried the doorknob. It was unlocked.

As Singleton threw the door open, Perry rushed into the darkness and leaped upon the bed. His knife-hand stabbed downward again and again. Finally he sat back on the bed, exhausted.

"He's finished," Perry said.

"Good work, Perry," Barlow chuckled. "This sure was easy, wasn't it fellahs?"

Suddenly a voice from a corner of the room said, "Looking for me, boys?"

For a moment the three intruders froze in place.

There was a gunshot and Perry fell across the bed. Barlow and Singleton darted out into the hall. The ramrod got in front of his man as they ran down the hallway. Another shot rang out and Singleton grunted. His knees buckled and he fell face first on the floor.

Barlow reached the stairs and took them down in two leaps. He sprinted into the alley and vaulted into his saddle.

He left Jaggersville as fast as he could ride. For the first time in a long time he felt fear. The bullet that hit Perry had passed only inches from his head. His ears still rang from the gun's blast.

He might need help on this job.

7.

The stranger stood in the hallway in front of his room. The shooting had awakened some of the customers yet no one poked their heads out to take a chance of getting shot in the crossfire. Moments passed and the quiet settled back in. A dog barked on the street. Brazos could hear the low, faint pounding of Barlow's horse as it rode away out of town.

He checked Perry, saw that he wasn't breathing, and went down the hallway to Singleton. He was alive. The stranger hoisted him up, dragged him back into the room, and laid him on the bed. He was wounded in the shoulder.

"Can you talk?" the stranger asked.

"Yeah," Singleton said.

"Was it worth it?"

"Right now I'd say no."

"You mind tellin' me the deal?"

"He's after you and the others," Singleton said.

"Venters?"

"Yeah," Singleton replied. He groaned and held his arm.

The stranger took Perry's knife and cut a strip from the bedsheet. He used it to bind Singleton's wound.

"Want a smoke?"

Singleton nodded and the stranger rolled them both a cigarette and lit them.

"Why me? Because I was with the kid?"

Singleton nodded. "Yeah."

"It was self-defense."

"It don't matter to Venters what it was. Nothin' matters ta him once he sets his mind on somethin'. He's like thet. He'll have Barlow kill the kid and anyone around him. It don't matter who."

"That's crazy!"

"All he knows is thet one of his men's been kilt and it's his duty to take care of it. He feels he can't let it pass."

"And he wants revenge?"

"Yep. An eye fer an eye. Thet's his code."

They sat quietly and smoked for a while.

"Get me down to the doc's place, will ya, friend?" Singleton groaned. "I don't feel so good."

"Sure," the stranger said.

The stranger helped the wounded man stand. They went down the stairs to the street. He put an arm around the man's waist and walked him up the road to the doctor's office.

"Doc Arnold don't ever lock his door," Singleton said as they stood there. "I kin make it from here."

"You sure about that?"

Singleton nodded then said, "About the Bar T. Venters is gonna go after anybody out there who was in on the killing of Trask. Arny Trask meant a lot ta him."

"They'll have to deal with it, then, I guess," the stranger said.

"Yeah, but when Venters kills a Bar T cowboy, it'll turn into a shootin' war, and Venters has a small army of gun slingers."

"It happens all the time," the stranger said. "Let the Marshal deal with it."

"He can't. He's afraid of Venters and there's two wimin out at the Bar T who's gonna git hurt."

The stranger let that sink in for a moment.

"What do you care what happens to them?"

"I met Fanny Templeton once. I wouldn't want her to get hurt."

"Then you'd better go out there and help her."

Singleton shook his head. "Not me, friend. As soon as I get the doc to fix me up, I'm headin' south. It ain't healthy fer me around here no more. You don't know Venters like I do."

The stranger took out his Colt and checked the cylinder. He put in two bullets, closed it, and put it back. He stared at the wounded man.

"Where is it? The Bar T?"

"About ten miles east on the coach road. There's a big, dead tree where they used ta hang rustlers. You turn left there at the crossroad. It'll take you to the Bar T."

The stranger nodded and walked away. He went to the hotel for his saddlebag and got on his horse. The horse was glad to see him.

"Let's go out to the Bar T," the stranger said. "There's some oats waiting there for you, old pal."

8.

It came on slowly and quietly, starting with the stares and quiet whisperings at church. That graduated into giggles and chuckles.

Ella Templeton wasn't all that surprised, what with her own dull appearance. She wore men's overalls, shirts, boots, and she milked cows, too. She rode like a cowboy and could fire a gun. That's how she was raised.

When she first met and married Fred Dayton, their life had been good. But right after Fanny was born Fred seemed to lose interest in her and the ranch. He was from Ohio, originally, and was a very handsome charming man of the world and he had dazzled her and swept her off her feet. She had never thought of herself as beautiful or even pretty. Face-paint couldn't change that, so she wore none.

She did have a dress, but only one. She wore that once a year to the Flying R yearly barn dance. Tobey Reynolds, the Flying R owner, usually danced with her just to make his wife Mildred jealous. He was seventy-five.

When her husband was shot one night on the way back from town, Ella wasn't all that surprised. There was talk about another woman, a woman Fred had charmed away from her cowboy boyfriend. When Fred was found dead on the coach road outside Jaggersville, and the cowboy nowhere to be found, it looked like a simple case of jealous rage and revenge.

Ella Templeton-Dayton waited a respectful year then changed her name back to Templeton, the name of one of the earliest families to settle in Dark River Valley.

Ella Templeton's family had owned the Bar T for two generations. At first it was as large as the others but that slowly changed as ranchers like Cal Venters of the Circle V began to buy off their neighbors. Calvin Venters, the head of the Cattlemen's Association, was very aggressive in pursuing his dream of owning all of Dark River. One time he even put a fence across the back road into town claiming it was on his land. It took the efforts of the town lawyer, Eli Meyers to get a court order to take it down. Venters backed off on that one but held a grudge against Meyers ever since then.

Another time Venters had successfully, if illegally, fenced off a stream that ran in a straight line north to south, along the west boundary of his land. He merely moved a portion of his fence a few feet to the west to close the stream off from six smaller spreads. This act of disregard caused such an outcry that Venters quickly moved the fence back to its original position.

Everyone in the Dark River Valley Basin feared and disliked Cal Venters.

Except the Owl Hawks.

They were a secret band of vigilantes who took matters into their own hands and started tearing down Venter's fences when they violated the law and closed off free-rangeland and water sources. There were certain rules, not laws on the books, but rules of behavior that had been established in the past. These rules held that neighbor was to respect neighbor. A law was not needed for that. It was for mutual survival.

But Venters seemed to have forgotten all about that. He hired only the meanest, toughest, most aggressive hands he could find. Those found sympathetic to the other ranchers were quickly cut loose.

One such cowboy was Bob Harnell, a young cowboy from down around the San Antonio River. He quickly left

Venter's Circle V and went to work for the Bar T. By the time he signed on to ride for it, the Bar T was down to twenty square miles of range and five thousand head of cattle. To make it worse, Ella Templeton was a widow with only seven cowhands and no ramrod.

So when her new hand, Bob Harnell walked up from the bunkhouse in the morning with a stranger by his side, Ella Templeton and her daughter came out on the front porch to look.

"I've got us a new hand, Mrs. Templeton," Harnell said.

"Oh, do you now?" Ella Templeton replied, staring at the young man fidgeting nervously in front of her. "And what is your name, young man?"

Cole removed his hat. He looked around.

"It's Ed Cole, ma'am," Harnell said before Cole could answer.

"I see. Can you talk, Mr. Cole or does Mr. Harnell have to do it for you?"

"No, ma'am," Cole said. "I kin talk."

"Where are you from, Mr. Cole?"

"Wyomin', ma'am."

"And are you a cowboy?"

"Yes, ma'am. I am," Cole said.

"How old are you, sir?"

"I'm not sure. Twenty, I reckon."

Ella Templeton smiled and nodded. "You're a long way from home, aren't you?"

"Well, sort of, I guess."

While Ella Templeton stared at the young man, he had his eyes fixed on young Fanny.

"I can't pay much, Mr. Cole," Ella said, "but all your meals will be free and I'm pretty good at patching up bruises and sprains. Do you have your own horse and saddle?"

"What was thet, ma'am," Cole said. He hadn't heard.

"He has, ma'am," Bob Harnell said.

"I do," Cole said.

Mrs. Templeton laughed. "Well, Mr. Harnell, would you please call the boys up from the bunkhouse for breakfast?"

"Yes ma'am." Harnell left the kid standing alone.

"Did Mr. Harnell tell you what's going on with Mr. Venters, Mr. Cole?"

"Some, ma'am."

"And you still want to hire on?"

"Yes ma'am." The kid looked down at his feet.

"Look at me, Mr. Cole," she said sharply. "I've had over a dozen cowboys ride away because they were afraid of Venters' ramrod, Mr. Barlow. Are you that easily scared off that you'll run like a rabbit?"

The kid looked up at Ella Templeton. "My name is Ed Cole, ma'am, and I don't run scared from nobody."

For a moment they held each other's gaze.

"Then you are welcome to my home, Mr. Cole. Please come in and have breakfast with us."

9.

The stranger rode slowly east on the old coach road thinking about what the lawyer Eli Meyers and the doctor told him about Venters. It seemed that Cal Venters was a wrathful and revengeful man. He would avenge the death of his cowboy Arny Trask, no matter how many people got hurt in the process. And now he, the stranger, had killed another of his men, Perry. That made two in one day. Venters would be furious with rage.

Now that he knew Venters would be coming after the Bar T cowboy Bob Harnell and the kid from Wyoming, he figured he should just ride out to the Bar T and warn them, and then ride on. He was finished in Jaggersville. It wasn't safe for him there or anywhere near the Circle V Ranch.

He'd seen this kind of thing before. It would end badly for everyone. Only the law could stop it, and sometimes not even it could. In some cases the law sided with the most powerful. Range wars were easily started, and once started, very hard to stop. He wanted no part of it.

He saw the big, dead tree up ahead in the early morning light. When he got there he turned left. The sun was coming up fast. About five miles on he saw the ranch house in the distance. Smoke rose up from the chimney. A few crows were circling around it and the bunkhouse. As he came up into the yard he saw hens and roosters roaming free.

He dismounted just inside the fence and led his horse down to the barn. He could hear voices in the house and smell bacon. He let his horse loose to find hay and water, then, walked back up to the ranch house and onto the porch. A girl came out to meet him.

"Can I help you, sir?"

"Is Mr. Harnell and Mr. Cole around?"

"Ask the man in to breakfast, Fanny," Ella Templeton called out to them.

"Thet's my mom," Fanny Templeton said. "We're just having breakfast. Please come in, sir."

As the stranger went into the house with her, she asked, "Are you a salesman, sir?"

The stranger chuckled. "No, ma'am."

"Oh." She sounded disappointed.

He followed her through the foyer, chuckling to himself.

They went into the kitchen. There were seven cowboys and the kid sitting around the long plank kitchen table eating. He smelled the coffee.

Ella was at the stove. She turned, saw the stranger, and stared at him. They locked eyes for a moment. He smiled and took off his hat.

"I hope I'm not intruding, ma'am," the stranger said.

"Coffee?" Ella said, as if they were friends.

He said, "Yes, ma'am."

She got another tin cup from the sideboard and poured hot coffee and gave it to him. She piled some scrambled eggs, grits, and bacon on a tin plate and offered that too.

"Much obliged, ma'am," he said and sat down next to the kid and Harnell. Everyone looked at this man dressed in a suit. He was no cowboy. A few snickered.

"He said he's looking for Mr. Harnell and Mr. Cole," Fanny said. She went and stood beside her mother near the stove.

"Well, there they are, sir," Ella said.

"He knows us ma'am," the kid said. "We've met."

The stranger looked at Ella Templeton.

"Ma'am, did Mr. Harnell tell you about last night, when Mr. Cole shot and killed Arny Trask in the Skinny Lady during a poker game, using Mr. Harnell's gun?"

Ella Templeton looked at Harnell. "Is that true, Mr. Harnell?"

"Yes ma'am." Bob Harnell cringed a little.

"Do you know what that means, Mr. Harnell?"

"Yes ma'am. It means Mr. Venters will send his men out here to kill me and Mr. Cole."

"Yes, I'm sure he will."

"It was self-defense," the stranger said. "Trask was going to shoot Mr. Cole. Mr. Cole was unarmed."

"Unarmed in the Skinny Lady Saloon? That wasn't very smart of you, Mr. Cole."

"No, ma'am."

"Where was your gun?"

"Ah, it's a long story, Mrs. Templeton."

"And interesting too, no doubt."

"Venters' men will be coming," the stranger said.

Ella Templeton sighed in resignation. "I suppose I'll have to fire you both or hide you or just hand you over to Venters." She paused a moment. "But I can't do that."

"Why not?" Ed Cole asked.

"Because, Mr. Cole, they would either hang you or drag you behind a horse. Either way, they will kill you two, and I wouldn't be able to sleep nights if they did."

"The kid and I will ride off," Harnell said. "That should take care of it, ma'am."

"I don't think so," the stranger said.

"Why not?"

"Venters will think the lady here is hiding you. Maybe his men will come in and burn the barn down or kill a few cows. He'll have his men hang around here day and night. This lady's life will never be the same until he's satisfied you two are dead. And even then he'll hold a grudge against Mrs. Templeton."

"Well, that about spoils my day, mister!" Ella chuckled.

"Brazos. Call me Brazos."

"Well, Mr. Brazos, what do you think I should do?"

"It's hard to say, ma'am," the stranger said. "Where is your husband?"

"I'm a widow, sir. It's just me and my daughter."

That did it. That's all it took. It was the code again. It seemed as if he was always running up against the code. He couldn't turn his back and walk away now.

"Ma'am," the stranger said. "My horse and I could use a little rest. We've been on the road for over a month now. I would really be obliged if you let us use your barn for a while. I'd be glad to pay. I've had enough of town."

"I know what you're doing, Mr. Brazos. It's most kind of you but you don't have to. It's not your problem."

The stranger chuckled. "Well, Mr. Cole and Mr. Harnell are poker players, and we poker players always stick together. Right, Mr. Cole? Mr. Harnell?"

"That's fer sure," Harnell said.

"I see," Ella Templeton said.

She felt trapped. No matter what move she made, Venters would come after the Bar T and her cowboys would get hurt. Some would be killed, and she didn't want that on her conscience.

Suddenly she was very glad the man called Brazos was there.

10.

It was dark. Venters and Barlow were on the porch talking. "First they kill Arny and then Perry. Singleton has disappeared. Who the hell are they?" Venters asked Slinger Barlow.

"From what I get from the boys it's just some kid from Wyomin' an' the cowhand from the Bar T. The gambler, too, of course."

"They killed my men and I can't let that stand. I want them all alive so I can hang them out there on that old tree by the Bar T. Just to let them know they can't get away with it."

"Yeah, boss, that would show 'em."

"Anything more on those fence breakers?"

"The Owl Hawks? Yeah. I found out thet Harnell, is one of 'em."

"Harnell! The cowboy who slipped the kid the gun that killed Arny?"

"Yeah, the Bar T cowboy."

"Maybe all the Bar T men are Owl Hawks," Venters said.

"That could be. I wouldn't be a bit surprised, boss."

"That would be all the excuse I need to put the Bar T out of commission and take that Templeton woman down a peg or two."

"I hate to tell you, boss, but Todd has been playin' around with her daughter."

"What? You sure?"

"Yep. He's stuck on her real good."

"I'll have to put a stop to that," Venters said. "And real quick."

After Barlow left for the bunkhouse Venters stood on the porch thinking. Finally he went into the living room where Beth sat reading on the sofa. Her ever-present cane was by her side. He stood looking down at her.

"Is Todd up in his room, dear?" Venters asked.

Beth stopped reading and looked up at him. "No dear, he's still out. He been keeping late hours lately. I can't guess for the life of me where he goes."

"I can."

Beth Venters placed her book down. "Oh? Where?"

"He's taken up with the Templeton girl."

"The Templeton girl? Really? Didn't she lose her father a few years ago?"

"Yes, a jealous lover shot him in the back. They're all poor trash and sinners, the whole lot of 'em."

"I met the mother once, in town. She seemed like a nice woman."

"She's trash and so is her daughter."

"Do you think so, dear?" She knew better than to argue with Cal. These days he was always in ill humor.

"Yes, I do."

"Well, dear," she said, "when Todd comes home, ask him what his intentions are. See if he is serious about the girl."

Venters nodded and went back out. He sat on the porch chaise and rolled a cigarette. He smoked while staring out into the night. He could hear voices from the bunkhouse.

Someone was playing an accordion and singing. He nodded off.

The next thing he became aware of was somebody coming up the porch steps. It was Todd.

"Father?"

Venters immediately went on the attack. "I know where you've been!" He never called the boy son or Todd. It was always you this and you that.

"Oh?" Todd said. "I guess you had someone follow me, then."

"You're not to see her anymore, is that clear?"

"Who's going to stop me father, you?"

"If I have to, yes, I will!"

Todd Venters sighed. He stared at his father in the soft glow of the light from the house.

"Father, I know you never loved me an' wished I had died instead of James." James was the stillborn twin. "In your way of thinking I killed him and almost killed mother. I know that."

Cal Venters looked away, avoiding his son's stare.

"If that's what you think, then go ahead and think it," he said. "At least if James was alive I wouldn't be ashamed of him."

"Oh, father. How sad of you to say that. But thank you sir, for being so honest."

Suddenly Venters' temper kicked in.

"Get out of my sight! I can't stand the sight of you anymore! Just go!"

"Thank you, father," Todd said. His eyes were moist. He choked back tears. He went to the open door, looked in and shouted, "Good-bye, mother! I love you!"

The young man went down to the corral, saddled his horse, and in fifteen minutes rode out into the night. A few minutes later his mother, using her cane for support, came slowly out onto the porch.

"Was that Todd, dear?"

"Yes."

"Did he just say good-bye?"

"Yes. Go back in, dear, you'll catch cold."

"Is he coming back, dear?"

"No, dear."

"Oh." Beth Venters seemed disoriented. She turned and went back into the house.

11.

Some years before hiring on at the Circle V, Slinger Barlow kept questionable company. In fact, he ran with an outlaw gang called the Springer Boys. They operated along the Platte River in Nebraska and Wyoming, robbing banks and trains. One day they got caught in an ambush. Barlow escaped but was severely wounded by a railroad guard sharpshooter. He almost died.

When he got back on his feet, Barlow dodged the law by making his way south through Nebraska, across Kansas and into the Texas panhandle, working as a cowboy.

When he hit Jaggersville, in the Dark River Valley, he met up with a hard-drinking, hard-riding cowboy who worked for the meanest rancher in the valley. This rancher only hired the hardest and roughest cowboys, cowboys who weren't afraid to step on other people's toes, cowboys who were loyal to the brand. This cowboy took Barlow to meet his boss, Calvin Venters. Venters hired Barlow and a year later he was ramrodding the Circle V Ranch.

Barlow really never took to Venters because the man was distant and exploded without warning. But he stayed on anyway because the pay was good and the Circle V was a safe place to hide out from the law in Nebraska. No one would look for him in a one- horse town like Jaggersville, Texas.

Also, being first-gun on a spread like the Circle V was a reward all in itself. It made Barlow feel important. He now had power and prestige. Putting up fences to close out the other ranches was Barlow's suggestion. He wanted barbed wire but Venters wasn't ready to go that far, thinking it was too dangerous to his own cattle.

At his boss's bidding, Barlow put fear into people's hearts. He was a strict enforcer and felt no remorse in following Venters orders, no matter how cruel or wrong.

The day after Todd left the Circle V, Venters called Barlow into his study to talk to him.

"Barlow, it's time you stopped playin' around and did something about those fence busters. It's gettin' pretty darn expensive as well as a pain in the ass."

"I know, boss," Barlow said. "I've been thinkin' about it and I've got it all figured out. I know how to stop these varmits right in there tracks."

"Well, it's about time," Venters growled. He wasn't happy. "And you'd best make a move real quick!"

"I already have, boss. I got three people comin' in an' they're real good at takin' care of problems like this."

"What kind of people?"

"Experts on matter sech as this, boss," Barlow said in confidence. "And they're real fast on the draw."

"What can they do that you can't do, Barlow?"

"Them bein' strangers hereabouts, an' their faces not known, they kin just go out there and brace Harnell and kill him and the kid."

"Are you certain they're in with the Owl Hawks?"

"Oh, yeah, I think all her cowboys are, boss, an' these three experts will put an end to thet!"

"It sounds good, but…"

"Don't worry, these experts will solve all yer problems with them Owl Hawks, then vanish."

Venters thought about Barlow's plan. It might work. He would not be connected in any way and that was important. But if the word got out it could cause him some trouble.

"You sure this will work, Barlow?"

"Trust me, boss. No one will know," Barlow said.

"Alright, fine."

"The only thing is they want the money up front."

Venters gave that some thought, then chuckled. "No, I don't do business that way. How much?"

"There'll be three of 'em. Five hundred each."

Venters considered that for a moment. "They'll get the money when I see 'em and not before. You think I'm a fool?"

Slinger Barlow shrugged.

"Alright boss. I'll be meeting them up in the panhandle. I'll be gone a few days."

"This better work, Barlow, or you're done here," Venters said bitterly. "You get that?"

"Sure, Mr. Venters, sure!" Barlow nodded. As he left he muttered under his breath, "An' maybe you're done too, boss."

12.

The next evening, after Barlow left, Cal Venters sat in his study brooding. Here he was, the most important man in the Dark River Valley and yet his life felt like an empty vessel. He would never have another son and he put the blame for that upon the one he did have. To him, Todd felt more like a curse than a blessing.

Todd had grown to hate him but Cal Venters never once considered the fault might be his own. He conceded nothing to no one when it came to who was to blame for what. It wasn't in him to say, "I'm sorry." He was a proud man. Worse than that, he was a very hubristic man, full of himself and power.

He wanted Todd to return with his tail between his legs, full of repentance and humility, a humility which he himself had never shown to anyone, but expected in others. He never once grabbed the young man, in his arms and said, "I love you son!" It just wasn't in him.

No, call Cal Venters was too hard a man to do that.

He sighed, stood up, looked around, and then went upstairs to the bedroom. Beth lay in bed reading a book. She looked pale and worn.

"The little ingrate is probably holed up in town in the whorehouse," Venters mumbled to himself. "I'll not beg him to come back."

"Perhaps you were too harsh on him, Cal," Beth said.

"Harsh on him? Ha! You've spoiled him, that's what!"

There it was again, the blaming game. "He's never done a hard day's work in his life! Run with the wolf pack is all he does. Drinking and fornicating with those low-life, no-good cowhands down at the Skinny Lady Saloon! That's all he's good for. And now it's that girl from the Bar T!"

"I wish he would get serious about some nice girl," Beth said. "Maybe then he'd settle down."

"Well, it won't be her. I'll see to that!"

"Come to bed, dear," Beth said. "You're tired."

"No, I can't sleep. I'll be in the study for a while."

Venters went down to the study and sat at his desk thinking, his mind jumping from subject to subject.

Finally his mind grabbed onto the Owl Hawks once more. They were a thorn in his side and caused him time and money in replacing the damaged fences. He also lost three men in running battles with them. He never knew where they were going to strike next.

He had been working with some political connections at the county level, trying to get them to pass a law to make destroying fences a felony punishable by five years in prison. One of his connections was writing up a bill to do just that. Once that happened, it would put a stop to the Owl Hawks.

But until then, the Circle V was left to its own devices. The town Marshal wasn't expected to do anything, and the County Sheriff had his hands full. That left the Texas Rangers, and they were too busy with rustlers and bank and train robbers. The Circle V would have to do the best it could on its own.

He was in his study when, just before midnight, one of his cowhands came in to see him.

"What is it, Harding?" he asked. When Barlow was away, Harding took over as ramrod.

"Someone wants to talk to you about the fence busters, Mr. Venters," Harding said.

Venter's heart started to race.

"Bring him in, Harding."

"Yes sir."

The man came in. He was a cowboy from the Double R spread. Venters stared at him.

"Are you one of them?" he demanded.

"I was. I've had enough," the man said. "I'm headin' north. I need a little extra cash, maybe five hundred?"

Venters stared hard at the man. "Do you have names?"

"Not unless I have to."

Venters got the money from the safe and put it on the table. The cowboy stared at it.

"Alright then, what have you got?"

"The place of the next raid. Tomorrow night they're gonna hit the fence up at the rock quarry, where the stream runs across."

"What time?"

"Sometime after mid-night."

"Who's the boss?"

"There ain't no boss. Just a bunch of ass holes getting' drunk 'n raisin' hell."

"Are you kidding?"

"Kidding?" the cowboy chuckled. "No sir, I ain't."

Venters went back to the safe and got another bank certificate and put it on the desk. The man stared at it

"Give me two names, for a hundred more."

The man thought it over then shrugged. "Hell, why not? Bob Harnell and Rudy Adams."

Venters nodded. Harnell was the Bar T cowboy who was involved in the shoot-out with his man Arny Trask.

How would you like to make an extra five hundred?"

"Hell, fer that I'd squeal on my own pappy!"

Venters chuckled. "Good, I like that. I want you to go with my men tomorrow. Show them the exact spot. When it's over, you'll get the extra five hundred, and you can ride away a rich man."

"Sure," the cowboy said.

Venters thought about what this meant. It was the big break he had been waiting for and now it was here.

Venters turned to Harding. "Our friend here is going to spend the night down at the bunkhouse. See that he's treated right." The cowboy picked up his money.

After they had left, Venter poured himself a drink. He suddenly felt very good.

"To the end of the Owl Hawks," he said to himself. "I finally have them right where I want them!"

The more he thought about it the more excited Venters became. Perhaps he should take charge of the ambush himself. He and Harding could handle this thing without Slinger Barlow and his three experts. He was getting tired of Barlow anyway. Maybe he should replace him with Harding. Yes, the more he thought about it the better he liked it. He had never really liked Barlow all that much. Once the Owl Hawks were dealt with and out of the way, he'd send Barlow packing.

Venters visualized the future. His name would appear on the front page of the Jaggersville Gazette as the hero of the day, the man who had stopped the Owl Hawks. All the other big ranchers would look up to him.

He would have liked Todd to be at his side. This was something the unruly and wild boy would love to get involved in. The kid was a man, now. He could ride and shoot with the best of them. All of a sudden, Todd wasn't so bad after all.

13.

After the fight with his father, Todd Venters rode into Jaggersville, stopped at the Skinny Lady Saloon for a bottle of rotgut, and took it to the Royal Hotel where he got very drunk. He slept until evening of the next day and awoke with a pounding hangover. As the only cure for a hangover is a little hair of the dog that bit you, he went back to the Skinny Lady Saloon for a drink.

He bought another bottle of whiskey, found an empty table in the shadows, and sat down. He was already half in the bag from last night's binge.

Ten minutes later six cowboys came in and sat at a nearby table. Thinking they were alone, they drank, smoked, and talked. Sometimes they mentioned his father's name. He listened for a while then took his chair and bottle over and squeezed into a narrow spot between two of them.

For a moment they froze and stared in surprise. Here was young Todd, Venters' son, as if he had dropped out of the sky, sitting amongst them. Most of them knew him as a wild, good-natured, rebellious kid who didn't get along well with his father. They also saw that he was a bit drunk.

"Hi, Todd," Bob Harnell said.

Todd stared at Harnell, trying to focus his whiskey-soaked eyes. "Say, don't I know you? Yer Harnell, aincha? My daddy is lookin' for you, Harnell. You and the rest of the Bar T boys. He's gonna plow you all under."

"What about you, kid," Rudy Adams said. "Who you lookin' for?"

"Me? I ain't lookin' for nobody, Adams," Todd said in an off-key voice.

Harnell cut in, saying, "Naw! Ol' Todd is okay. He's a good friend of the Bar T, aincha, Todd? Especially a certain young woman out there. Right, Todd?"

"Right an' nobody better not say anything about her," Todd said. "She's an angel."

They all nodded in agreement.

"Been drinking, have ya, kid?" Tim Husker asked.

"Maybe, what's it to ya?"

"No offense, kid, just askin'."

Lambeth chuckled. "He sure has. Don't nobody light a match or the kid will go up in flames!"

They all chuckled.

"Yer all Owl Hawks, ain't ya?" Todd blurted out.

"What makes ya think that, kid," Wes Stoner asked.

"I heard ya talkin, about my ol' man."

The cowboys stared at Todd Venters wondering what the next move should be.

"Does that bother you, friend?" Harnell asked.

The young man chuckled. "Hell no! I could care less about the son of a bitch!"

"You two had a fight agin'?" Adams asked.

"Agin'? Hell, we ain't never stopped," Todd said.

They still had their eyes fastened on the boy. Ben Madden looked at Husker and said, "Whatta we gonna' do with him? We can't let this pass. He's heard too much."

"Take him outside, Madden," Wes Stoner said. "Make sure he don't come back."

"Yeah, okay," Madden said.

Harnell put his hand down by his gun. "No you ain't. Lay a hand on the kid and I'll ventilate ya!"

Madden glared at Harnell. "Who made you boss?"

"It ain't about bein' boss," Harnell said coldly, "It's about me and the kid bein' friends, Madden. If you don't like it, you better slap leather right now!"

Madden put his hands on the table. "Alright, then he's your problem, and you better fix it. We ain't got all night."

Harnell turned to Todd. "You wanna be an Owl Hawk, kid?"

"Hell, yes!"

"Alright, then," the cowboy said. He raised his glass, "Boys, let's drink to the newest member of the Owl Hawks." They all drank. Todd giggled happily.

"Let's ride," Husker said.

They stood up, watching as Todd struggled unsteadily to his feet. Harnell put an arm around his waist and they all walked outside to the horses. Marshal Spears came out of nowhere. He stopped.

"Is that you, Todd?" Spears asked.

"No, Marshal," Todd said. "It's my ghost you dumb ass!" The boy giggled drunkenly.

"Ah, we'll take care of him, Marshal," Husker said.

The Marshal nodded. "You do that, Tim. And see no harm comes to the boy. I don't want no trouble from his father." With that, the Marshal walked away.

"Kin you ride, kid?" Harnell asked.

Todd suddenly threw up in the road. He inhaled the crisp night air. It somewhat revived him. He nodded and mounted his horse. The others did the same. They rode slowly out of town. Harnell kept a close eye on Todd, riding behind him.

"Where's Dobbs?" someone asked.

"He said he didn't feel too good," Madden said.

They rode on.

The longer they rode the more revived Todd seemed. The air was chilly and crisp. He drank it in, inhaling deeply. Harnell came up beside him.

"Feelin' better?" Todd nodded. They rode on.

In two hours they came up to a fence and followed it for several miles. Then beyond, on the other side of it, they could hear the sound of water running fast and hard over rocks. On the same side as the stream, about thirty yards back of it, was the remains of an old stone quarry.

The Owl Hawks slowed down then stopped a good ways back from the fence. Rudy Adams nudged his horse a bit closer. The night was quiet. Too quiet.

Harnell put a hand on young Todd Venter's arm and motioned for him to move back into the shadow of a lone pine tree.

"Somethin' is fishy," he whispered to the boy. "Don't move."

Suddenly Adams raised his hand and pointed at the fence and they all walked their horses up to it.

"Somethin' ain't right here," Lambeth said.

"Yeah, it's too damn quiet, if ya ask me," Stoner said.

"Hell," Husker said in a loud voice, "let's do it!"

Just as Madden tossed a rope out at a fence post, rifles roared in the night. The flash of muzzles could be seen behind the pile of rocks. A fusillade of bullets hit their targets and the Owl Hawks jerked and twisted in their saddles. They were cut down by bullets from thirty repeating Winchester rifles on Venters' side of the fence.

"Oh, God!" Harnell screamed. He grabbed the bridle of Todd Venter's horse.

Someone on the other side of the fence shouted, "Don't let those two get away!" Todd Venters knew it was his father's voice bellowing in the night like an angry bear.

Rifles barked and bullets shattered the pine tree beside them. Harnell tried to get the horses turned and pointed away from the fight.

"Kill those two!" Cal Venters' voice rang out again.

Harnell finally got the horses pointed away from the carnage. He smacked the kid's mount on its flank and sent it galloping away. Then he spurred his own mount out front and took the lead. Miles on, they could still hear the rifles firing behind them. After a while there was only the wind and the howling of a coyote far in the distance. They slowed down and rode side by side.

"Where?" Todd asked.

"The Bar T," Harnell said, gasping for air.

"We shoulda stayed an' fought back," Todd said.

"You'd be dead, if we did," Harnell said. He groaned.

"You're hit, Harnell!"

"Yeah, I guess so."

"Kin you make it to the Bar T?"

"I ain't a goin' there. I'd only cause Mrs. Templeton more trouble. She don't need thet."

They came up on a hill overlooking the ranch house and stopped to look down at it. The windows were dark in both the house and the bunkhouse.

"You gotta get fixed up, Harnell. You're bleedin' bad."

"Don't worry about me, kid." Harnell coughed, and then groaned. "Some lucky bastard sure winged me good."

For a moment the two young cowboys looked at each other. Harnell swayed in the saddle. Todd reached out but Harnell pushed his hand away.

"Do you love her?" Harnell said.

"Yeah, I do."

"So do I," Harnell said. "But she ain't fer me, Venters, she's fer you. An' it's fer you to protect her."

"I will, Bob. I will."

"Is thet a cowboy's promise?"

"It is."

A cold wind blew against them. They shivered.

"Then thet's good enough fer me, cowboy," Harnell said.

He groaned again and nudged his horse into a slow canter. Todd Venters sat in his saddle watching Harnell until he could no longer see him.

He turned his horse and rode down towards the Bar T. He stopped on a knoll and looked down for a moment then walked his horse slowly down to the back where the clotheslines were. Dismounting there, he led his horse over to the barn and put it in a stable with some water and oats, then sat in a corner on a pile of hay until sunrise.

Come sunrise he would go to the house to see Mrs. Templeton.

14.

It was morning. In the kitchen, Ella Templeton listened as Todd Venters told her what happened the night before. When he finished she sighed.

"Where is Mr. Harnell now?"

"He's gone, ma'am," Todd said. "He said he didn't want to cause any problems for you and the Bar T. He was shot pretty bad. I suspect he's cashed his chips in."

Fanny began to cry softly.

Ella Templeton had a concerned look on her face. She stared at Todd. "I think you should go home, Todd. Your mother is probably very worried about you."

"I'll go home after this is over, if you don't mind, ma'am. I promised Bob Harnell I'd see this through with you."

"Alright," Ella said. "If you insist."

The stranger and Cole didn't say anything.

"More coffee, Mr. Brazos? Mr. Cole?"

The stranger chuckled. "Excuse me, ma'am," but I think we're all going to need something a little stronger."

"Oh, why?"

"Your cowboy Harnell was an Owl Hawk. They took down Venters' fences."

"Yes. I see."

"Will the Marshal come out to help you, if you ask him?"

"Yes, I think so."

"Then I'd send a man to do that, ma'am," the stranger said. "Get the law involved. Let the Marshal sort it out."

"Now?"

"As soon as you can, ma'am."

"Alright," Ella said, "I'll go down to the bunkhouse and send Mr. Brown into town to get him."

"Mr. Cole and I should go with you," the stranger said.

"Alright, if you want to."

After they were gone, Todd went to Fanny. "I sure missed you, Fanny Templeton."

"I missed you, too, Todd Venters."

"After this blows over, could I come an' court you right and proper?"

"Sure, if you kin get past my mom."

"Okay, I'll be sure ta butter her up first, then."

They sat at the kitchen table staring at each other.

They heard voices out in the yard. People were walking around. Finally a horse rode away. Ella, Ed Cole, and the stranger came back into the kitchen.

"Mr. Venters," Ella said, "It must have been a long night for you. I'll make you some ham and eggs and some grits."

"That's most kind of you, ma'am."

"And after that you can rest in the bunkhouse."

An hour later Todd Venters checked on his horse and curled up on a cot in the bunkhouse. When he awoke it was mid-afternoon. He walked up to the ranch house. He was hungry again.

15

It was around noon. Cal Venter's and Harding were in the study when Slinger Barlow, finally got back with his three specialists, Tanner, Griswald, and Pearson. They were a rough looking trio of cutthroats. Tanner, the oldest, was short and had a patch over his left eye. Griswald was chubby and had a bushy, red beard. Pearson was a skinny, tall skeleton with bulging blood-shot eyes. They all smelled of whiskey, cigarette smoke, and sweat.

"Why did you bring these men here, Barlow?"

"Relax boss, you said you wanted to meet 'em. And they jest couldn't wait ta see the great Cal Venters! They heard about what a great man you was, boss. You ain't never gonna see 'em agin, I promise."

"I'd best not, or you're in trouble, mister!"

"Sure boss, sure," Barlow said.

Not satisfied with chastising his ramrod, Venters started to brag about how he had led his men on an ambush that wiped out the notorious Owl Hawks, and buried their bodies under a pile of rocks at the quarry.

"Does the Marshal know about this?" Barlow asked.

"No, and he don't need too, not just yet," Venters snapped. "Let me worry about the Marshal."

"Sure, sure, boss," Barlow said calmly. He winked knowingly over at Tanner.

There was short awkward silence and Venters suddenly exploded. "Well, whatta you four standin' around for? Git out and do what I'm payin' ya to do!"

Barlow shrugged. "You want us ta go right now, boss? We been on the road fer days now. We need a few hours rest."

"I want this over and done with! Behind me! So git out there and do it, Barlow!"

"Sure, sure, boss," Barlow said, as if cowed.

"And when it's over, you kin ride out with yer friends!"

Slinger Barlow froze, a stern look clouded his face. "What's thet, boss?" His eyes narrowed.

Venters opened the study safe and took out five hundred dollars in bank certificates. He laid them on the study desk. Tanner and his two men were staring at the pile of money still in the safe.

"Harding is taking your place as ramrod on the Circle V Barlow," Venters said. "I'm payin' you off."

Barlow chuckled and looked at Harding. "Oh, he is, is he?"

"That's what I said."

Barlow drew his gun without warning and shot Cal Venters in the chest. The old patriarch gasped and slumped to the floor. Harding turned to run but was shot three times in the back by Tanner, Griswald, and Pearson.

"Clean out the safe," Barlow growled. He stared at Venters body. He shook his head. "You damn old fool. I was loyal to you fer ten years, and this is what I get?"

The other three were at the safe removing the rest of the money. They suddenly heard Beth Venters call down.

"Is everything alright, Cal dear?"

Barlow looked up at the study ceiling, and then yelled, "Yes, my love, everything is fine."

Griswald chuckled and started for the stairs. Barlow grabbed his arm.

"Where you think yer goin', Griswald?"

"Up there, ta finish her off."

"You touch her an' I'll drill you!" Barlow hissed. He had his gun out and aimed at Griswald's gut. "Nobody touches her. She's been like a mother to me!"

Griswald nodded and slowly backed off.

When they had all the money, Pearson said, "Let's head back up north."

"Yeah," Tanner said. "Good idea!"

"Alright, but we gotta go a bit west, first, to the Bar T Ranch. There's some unfinished business I gotta take care of."

"Who's out there?" Griswald asked.

"The sons a bitches thet killed Trask and Perry, two of my best men."

Tanner said. "To hell with 'em! You ain't ridin' fer this brand anymore, so let it be."

"I can't. It sticks in my craw," Barlow said. "They rode with me and I can't jest walk away like it never was. I owe it to 'em both."

"Hell," Griswald said. "Killin' a couple more ain't gonna take long. Let's git her done 'n head north like we never been here!"

16.

They were sitting in the kitchen drinking coffee when suddenly Ed Cole put his cup down and went into the hallway.

"Somebody is coming!" Fanny said.

"It's most likely Brown and the Marshal," Todd Venters offered.

"No," the kid from Wyoming called in, "it ain't."

He watched Barlow, Tanner, Griswald, and Pearson ride boldly into the front yard and stare at the house. Those in the kitchen went into the hallway to get a clearer view.

"Mrs. Templeton? I'd like ta see Bob Harnell and thet pig lover from Wyomin', ifn you don't mind." Barlow yelled.

No one in the hallway moved.

"And kid, if yer in there too, I jest did you a favor! I plugged yer dad!"

Todd started for the front porch but the stranger grabbed his arm. "Not a good idea."

"I'm gonna brace the son of a bitch," Todd growled.

Brazos pulled his gun and tapped the young man on the side of his head with the butt. Todd's eyes rolled up in his head and his knees folded. Ed Cole caught him and eased him to the floor.

"Keep him here," the stranger told Ella. He looked at Wyoming. "You sure are a lot of trouble, kid."

"I kin handle this dance by myself," Wyoming said. "You kin go out the back."

"What, and let you have all the fun?"

Barlow's voice boomed out in the yard again. "If you don't send 'em out, ma'am, then me an' my friends will have to come in ta git 'em. You won't like thet!"

"Please don't go out there!" Ella Templeton said. "Wait for the Marshal!"

"I'm afraid the Marshal won't be able to deal with these men," the stranger said. "I know what they are." He turned to the kid. "Ready, Wyomin'?" The kid nodded.

They both went outside into the yard. The four gunmen saw them and started to dismount.

"Never mind that," the stranger said.

Barlow and his men suddenly realized their mistake. Caught cold in the saddle, all four played it safe for the moment, knowing they had few options. The only way out was to draw or ride.

"Ain't I seen you someplace before, mister?" Tanner ask. He squinted at the stranger trying to place him in his memory.

"That might be," the stranger said. He sidestepped away from the kid, putting more space between them.

"You ever been to Santa Fe?"

"I've been lots of places, friend," the stranger said, smiling.

"Maybe you heard about me," Tanner said.

"Who are you?"

"Brady Tanner. I killed Red Hardy in a shoot-out. I guess you've heard of Hardy. He was the fastest draw in the territory."

"Oh? When did you do that?" the stranger asked.

"Two years ago in Dodge City."

"That's funny. I killed him a long time ago in a poker game in Cheneyville, Kansas."

Tanner drew. His shot took the stranger's hat off. The stranger's shot took him between the eyes and snapped him back off of his horse.

From then on it a free for all.

Pearson's shot nicked the kid in the ribs and the kid's shot hit him dead center in the chest. His horse bolted and bucked, sending Pearson's body cartwheeling to the ground. He landed in a heap.

The stranger went down on one knee in a crouch and shot upward just as Griswald fired down at him. Griswald's aim was off as his horse shied and his shot hit the stranger high up on his left shoulder. The stranger's shot took Griswald in the belly and he fell forward in the saddle, griping the horn. The stranger shot him once more and he went over and down with a thud.

Barlow concentrated on the kid. He snapped off a shot that grazed the kid's right temple. The kid didn't even blink. He shot Barlow twice in the chest. The man dropped off his horse like a cut-down tree. He was dead before he hit the ground.

It was a while before the echoes of the gunshots faded away. The stranger stood up and looked at the kid. He nodded.

"Nice shooting, kid."

Suddenly the kid turned pale. He put his gun in its holster, slapped a hand over his mouth, and ran down behind the bunkhouse to throw up out of sight. The stranger chuckled and reloaded his Colt.

Ella Templeton, Fanny, and Todd came rushing from the house. Ella was carrying a shotgun. She stood there staring at the bodies.

"My God!" Ella said. She came over to the stranger and put a hand on his arm. "You're hurt."

"It's not much."

They heard horses coming up the road. In a few minutes Brown and the Marshal came pounding into the yard. They dismounted. The Marshal stared at the bodies. The kid came back from the bunkhouse looking pale.

"Are we in trouble, Marshal?" the kid asked.

"Normally, yes," the Marshal said. "But in this particular situation, no." He looked at Todd. "Son, yer father's dead.

Before he died he scribbled a note sayin' Barlow and his pals here shot an' robbed him."

"My mother! Is she alright?"

"Yes, she's fine. She's been askin' for you."

The young man looked lost. He turned to Fanny.

"Go see yer momma, Todd. She needs you," she said softly.

"I'll come back when I can."

Todd Venters walked quickly down to the corral, saddled his horse, and rode away.

17.

Many people in the Dark River Valley Basin came to Cal Venters' funeral for various reasons. Some were glad he was dead, some couldn't believe it, and some had to see for sure. Others came out of respect for his wife, Beth, and her son Todd.

As funerals went, this one was fairly plain and simple. The Parson spoke eloquently about Cal Venters' many virtues. He went on for a long time then stepped aside for the lawyer, Eli Meyers. Meyers also heaped praise on Venters. He finally ceded the floor to Doc Arnold.

When the doctor was finished, the Parson asked if anyone else wanted to say a few words.

Young Todd Venters, who was in the front row with his mother, got up. He walked slowly over to where his father lay in repose in a plain casket. He stared down at him for a moment and turned to face the congregation and visitors.

Everyone knew about the hatred between father and son, and wondered what Todd would say.

The young man cleared his throat and finally spoke.

"My father, Calvin Venters, was a mean son of a bitch," the young man began. "When I was fifteen years old he yanked me out of school and put me on a horse and sent me to Kansas on a trail drive. The work almost killed me."

Todd paused a moment and stared at his mother a few feet away. They smiled at each other.

"It almost killed me, but it didn't. Instead, it made a man out of me. It taught me what it meant to be a real cowboy, true to the code. And I'm forever grateful to my father for doing that."

Todd stared over at the casket for a second time, and then chuckled.

"Yes, he was a mean son of a bitch and he hated me and I hated him. Or we pretended to. It really wasn't hate it was tough love. Before he died he scribbled a note meant for me. It said, 'I love you son."

The young man choked back tears for a moment. He wiped his eyes.

"He had never called me his son or ever said that he loved me while he was alive. But he finally did, on his own terms."

Todd looked around, smiling.

"Anyway, I just want ta say I'm proud to be the son of Cal Venters, the meanest son of a bitch in the valley." Todd paused again then said. "Is Mrs. Templeton here in church?"

No one spoke until a voice from the back, in the middle of the pews, yelled, "Yeah, she's here. Why?"

"Well, ask her if I kin marry her daughter Fanny!"

Everyone started to laugh. Finally the voice came back with, "She said yes!"

Everyone applauded.

Todd Venters sat down and that concluded the ceremonial phase of Cal Venter's funeral.

Later they buried him.

After that, things calmed down in the Dark River Valley Basin. There was no more fence cutting. Todd had made that unnecessary by taking down the fences that blocked the free range and watering holes. He also sent a dozen of the Circle V cowboys to work at the Bar T.

Ella Templeton asked Ed Cole to stay on as the new ramrod of the Bar T and the kid said he would.

Fanny and Todd soon got married.

There was a dance and reception at the Circle V Ranch. It was held in the huge barn behind the ranch house. There was food, music, and much toasting to the bride and groom.

The kid got to kiss Fanny Templeton-Venters. The groom didn't care too much for that.

"That's yer last one, kid," Todd Venters said. "You ain't getting' no more!"

"We'll see about that," Ed Cole said. Everybody laughed.

Ella Templeton wore a dress. She and the stranger sat on a bale of hay drinking cider punch.

"How can I thank you, Mr. Brazos. You and Mr. Cole saved our lives."

"It was my pleasure, ma'am," the stranger said. "Any decent man would have done the same."

"The Marshal said those three men were wanted for murder, robbery, and rape."

"If that's true, then I guess it was a lucky thing the kid and I were there." The stranger stared at Ella Templeton. "Ma'am, may I say you look real pretty in that dress?"

"Why, thank you, Mr. Brazos."

"Please call me Jack, ma'am."

"Alright, Jack."

"Would you care to dance with me, ma'am?"

"I would love to dance with you."

It was a slow waltz and they blended in with the other dancers. He held her gently. She put her head on his shoulder and leaned toward him. His arms tightened around her. She moved her face up, her mouth against his ear.

"If you feel like kissing me I wouldn't be offended," she whispered.

"Alright," he said, "but I'll have to kiss you again, later."

"Why again later?"

"When I say good-bye, in the morning, ma'am."

For a moment she was silent, then she whispered softly again in his ear. "Then you better make them both count."

"I'll do my best ma'am. I surely will."

They stopped mid-floor and he kissed her. Some people kept on dancing around them, too embarrassed to show they noticed. Others smiled and chuckled. Some decided to kiss, too.

It was a long waltz.

The End

About the Author

R. Annan is a seasoned and traveled author with many interests. As a career serviceman he served in Korea and Vietnam. He also completed a one-year course at the Defense Language Institute at Monterey, California, and graduated from the University of South Florida with a B.A. in Art and Art History. After taking a two-year course in screenwriting at the Hollywood Scriptwriting Institute, he established *The Old Time Radio Club Time Machine* as both a scriptwriter and an actor.

A Note from the Author

Thank you for reading my book. If you enjoyed it, would you please consider rating and reviewing it? I'd enjoy your feedback. Here is a link to my author's page on Amazon: www.amazon.com/author/rannan

Look for other books to appear soon. Thank you!